First Friend

Christobel Mattingley

Illustrated by Craig Smith

SCHOLASTIC INC.

New York Toronto London Auckland Sydney
Mexico City New Delhi Hong Kong Buenos Aires

For David, my first friend.

—*C.M.*

For Casey Russell.

—*C.S.*

ISBN 0-439-40496-7

12 11 10 9 8 7 6 5 4 3 2 1   2 3 4 5 6 7/0

Printed in the U.S.A.   40
First printing, March 2002

1
New School

Kerry had been to school for
two years. She had made
many friends. She liked her
teacher. And she had
learned to read.

Then, Kerry's father
changed his job.

Kerry's family moved to
another town, and Kerry
had to go to a different
school.

It was a much bigger
school. It was three stories
high. There were many
flights of stairs and long
hallways with dozens of
doors.

In Kerry's first school,
there were twenty children
in her grade. In the new
school, there were one hun-
dred about Kerry's age.

There were four first-

grade classes named after
the points of the compass:
North, South, East, and
West. Kerry was in South.

Kerry's new teacher said,
"I am Miss Bell." She was

short. Her hair was gray.
Kerry's other teacher had
been tall with golden hair
almost to her waist.

Miss Bell said, "Everyone, this is Kerry."

The other children smiled at her, but their faces were strange.

Kerry had always shared
a desk with friends, but
now she had one all to
herself. At her old school,
the desks had been
arranged in groups. Here,

they were arranged in two
horseshoes, one inside the
other.

First, they sang songs.
Miss Bell played the music.
There was a vase of cheer-

ful daffodils on the shelf by
the keyboard.

In Kerry's first school,
there had been a bowl on

the cassette cabinet, and
the class had planted
daffodil bulbs in it. Kerry
wondered if they were
blooming yet.

Kerry did not know any
of the songs. At the end,
Miss Bell said, "Teach us
one of your songs, Kerry."
But Kerry shook her head.

"Tomorrow, perhaps." Miss
Bell smiled kindly.

Next, they did math. Miss
Bell gave Kerry a box of red,
yellow, and green counting
blocks all for herself.

"At my school we shared blocks," Kerry said.

"We do it this way, by ourselves," the children said.

Then, Miss Bell said, "You may go to the library now."

2
A Long Way

The children hurried out
the door, down the long
hallway to the right.

They went across the
landing to the left, ran

down the stairs and across

another landing. They

passed an open door.

Kerry could see the

playground outside. But the

others went down some
more stairs.

They jumped the two bot-
tom steps.

To the right and straight

ahead were two more doors to the playground. But the children ran around the corner to the left.

To Kerry it seemed a very long way.

There were some more

doors with the sound of recorders coming from behind
them. From another door
came the sound of computers.

The children disappeared
through a quiet door.

Kerry followed.

3
Old Friends

A lady smiled at Kerry and said, "I am Mrs. May, the librarian. This is your first day, isn't it?"

"It's my first day here,"
said Kerry, "but I've been to
school before, of course."

"Of course," said Mrs. May.
"Do you like reading?"

"Of course," said Kerry.

"Then come here often to read and exchange your books. And you may borrow books to take home

whenever you like. We keep
your library card at this
desk."

"Thank you," said Kerry.
She looked around the

room. It was much bigger than the library at her old school. All around the walls were shelves and shelves of books, many more books than in her old school library.

There were books about
trains and turtles, horses
and helicopters, dinosaurs
and dolphins, mice and
mountains.

There were books on how
to make things. There were
books on how to do things.
Kerry thought that there
must be a book on every
subject under the sun.

Then, on a low shelf
beside a big red rug, Kerry
saw all her favorite books:
*Where the Wild Things Are,
Winnie the Pooh, Peter
Rabbit, Willy, Corduroy,*

The Rainbow Fish, Babar, and *Each Peach Pear Plum* were all there.

The Very Hungry Caterpillar was there. And so were *Madeline* and *Ping.*

Kerry was among friends
again. She gathered them
into her arms and sat down
on the red rug.

The only books she left on

the shelf were *Arthur, Spot,*
Hairy Maclary, and *Harry*
the Dirty Dog. Kerry did not
like dogs.

The other children chose

their books. Mrs. May
waved her wand over
their library cards. They
put their books in their
bags.

A bell rang, but Kerry did not hear it.

"Good-bye," said Mrs. May. "It's time for you to go. Come back soon."

The other children left.

But Kerry lay on the red rug with her friends.

No one knew she was there.

4
Which Way

Mrs. May came to put away
some books. She found
Kerry. "Still here? It's time
for you to go."

Kerry stood up slowly.

It was hard for her to leave
her friends.

"You may take one with
you," Mrs. May said.

It was hard to choose.

"What about *Arthur* or
Harry?" asked Mrs. May.

Kerry shook her head.
She did not like dogs.

"Do you know the way
back?"

Kerry nodded.

But outside the library
door she stopped.

The hallway went left. It
went right. It stretched long
and empty, empty of people
but full of sound.

There were sounds of
recorders from behind the
doors where people played.
There were sounds of
computers behind the door

where people typed.

At both ends there were
doors with glimpses of grass
and trees.

Kerry turned left.

In the distance, she could
see stairs going up. She
walked to the stairs.

A big black dog climbed
down the stairs.

Kerry stopped and stood
still. She did not like dogs.

5
Black Dog

The black dog jumped the
two bottom steps. It came
up to Kerry.

Kerry stood very still. She
could feel its hot breath on

her hand. A drip from its
mouth dropped on her
shiny, black shoe.

She darted to the stairs.
The black dog jumped in
her way, right in the middle
of the stairs.

Kerry tried to hurry to
one side.

The black dog barked and
moved in front of her.

Kerry moved to the other

side. The black dog moved,
too. It moved the same way.

Kerry turned around. She
hurried back down the long
hallway.

The black dog followed.

Kerry came to another
flight of stairs. The black
dog passed her. It started to
walk up the stairs, its tail
waving like a flag.

Kerry heard footsteps
echo down the hallway.

She looked around. Mrs.
May was walking away
toward the other end.

Kerry turned back. She
ran as quickly as she could,
as quietly as she could,
after Mrs. May.

She reached the bottom of the stairs.

Mrs. May had gone. But the black dog was there again, on the second step.

Kerry said, "Go away,

dog." Her voice was swal-

lowed by the stairwell.

The black dog barked.

Kerry turned and ran.

The black dog was at her
heels. As she reached the
other stairs, the black dog
ran past her.

6
New Friend

Miss Bell was coming down the stairs.

"I thought you might be lost. It's such a big school, so many stories and so

many stairs, such long hallways and so many doors,"
she said.

"But Black Dog has found
you." She patted the black
dog.

Kerry said, "He barked
at me. He stopped me
from going up the
stairs."

Miss Bell said, "He knew
they were not the right

stairs. He knew you had lost your way."

Kerry asked, "Is he your dog?"

"Yes." Miss Bell smiled.
"Of course he should not
be at school, but he is
always so lonely at home by

himself on the first day

after summer vacation."

She patted him again.

"He follows me to school.

He likes looking after
children on their first day.
He likes making new
friends."

"He is my first friend
here," Kerry said. She

patted his back very lightly
and quickly.

Black Dog wagged his tail.

"He is my first dog friend."

"It is playtime now," Miss

Bell said. "Black Dog will take you outside. He will show you where the other children are playing."

Black Dog ran up the

stairs. Kerry followed.
Together they went out the
door to the playground.

Black Dog and Kerry ran
across the grass.

"Hello, Kerry! Hello, Black

Dog!" the children called.

"Come and play with us."

They all joined in a game together.